To America—Nation of Immigrants

This book belongs to: _____

Date: _____

Printed and bound in the United States of America.
First printing 2009.

Library of Congress Cataloging-in-Publication Data

Alexander, Keely.
    Davy Brown discovers his roots / written by Keely Alexander & Velani Mynhardt Witthöft ; illustrated by Manuela Pentangelo.
        p. cm.
        Summary: Davy Brown uses many resources to create his family tree of flags for a class assignment.
        ISBN-13: 978-1-60131-053-8
        [1. Genealogy—Juvenile fiction. 2. Emigration and immigration—Juvenile fiction. 3. Multiculturalism—Juvenile fiction. 4. Family—Juvenile fiction.]
        I. Witthöft, Velani Mynhardt. II. Pentangelo, Manuela, ill. III. Title.
                                                                        2009924097

Photographs of Keely Alexander and Velani Mynhardt Witthöft were taken by Corrynn Cochran.

115 Bluebill Drive

Savannah, GA 31419

(888) 300-1961

Published with the assistance of Dragonpencil.com

Keely Velani LLC gratefully acknowledges Benjamin Johnson, Claire Tesh, Elizabeth Stinebaugh, Robert Cohen, Randall Caudle, Chris McCammon, Gustav Witthöft, Peggy King Anderson, Sharalynn Cromer, and Jennifer Schouten for their contribution to this book.

DAVY BROWN
DISCOVERS HIS ROOTS

Written by Keely Alexander & Velani Mynhardt Witthöft

Illustrated by Manuela Pentangelo

A Keely Velani LLC Book
SEATTLE

Keely Velani.

Davy Brown was stumped by his own family tree. Sure, he was the star of the Ballard Vikings, but even for him this assignment was a curveball. How was he, Davy Brown, supposed to create a family tree of flags when he was just an American? He could already imagine his friends' exciting stories and colorful trees. His bare little tree would look so plain with one lone flag waving from the branches. His mom was from Boston, his dad from Seattle. His grandparents retired in Miami and Austin.

Immigration didn't have anything to do with him; he was pretty sure. But an assignment was an assignment, and he knew the rules: school first, baseball second. There'd be no pitching if his grades weren't passing. Davy figured there was only one way to get un-stumped: dig up the roots of his tree!

But then the bell rang. The digging will just have to wait, Davy thought. It was time for lunch, and lunch was his favorite period. That was when he and Carlos talked baseball. He rounded the cafeteria door and slid into the table as if he was sliding into home plate. Carlos was already seated, and the new girl from Mexico was sitting next to him. "*¿Cómo están amigos?* How's the teriyaki?"

"The chicken was slightly on the dry side, the rice a tad too sticky, and the coleslaw was as wilted as dead flowers," Carlos reflected, tapping his chopsticks on the table. "In hindsight, I should've gone with the pizza."

Davy peered at the coleslaw; it did resemble dead flowers. In fact, he thought it looked a lot like his mom's tulips in the back yard. Then his eyes stumbled upon the social studies and genealogy books stacked between Carlos's and Estella's lunch trays. Why so many books? he thought. It's only coloring in your family tree. "Are you all done with your project?"

Carlos patted his well-organized binder. "My research is complete. You know I like to have everything done well before the deadline."

Davy gulped. He hadn't even started his yet.

"Now, I'm just helping Estella."

Estella peeked out from her book. "Because I still learn English," she said in a soft voice.

"She's only been here for thirty-five days." Carlos liked to keep his numbers straight.

"Mi *padre* work in an orchard, but we go back soon," Estella added, feeling brave.

"And someday I might have to go back too," Carlos said hesitantly. This was something he'd never told Davy.

"What do you mean? You won't stay?" Davy tried to imagine who'd catch his fastballs when Carlos was gone, but he couldn't. We've been striking out batters together since kindergarten, he thought.

"Well, my father got a job here that paid more. He's an accountant. But it's only temporary," Carlos said, fidgeting with his binder. "Davy, what's the matter? You look upset."

Davy didn't want to admit that the thought of losing his best friend was overwhelming. "I don't know where to start on this stupid assignment. How much research does Ms. Fortuna expect me to do? My family is just American."

"Try the library or the Internet. I'm sure you can dig up something," Carlos said, trying to comfort his best friend.

"Internet!" Davy gasped. "I'm late! I have to meet Amit in the computer lab." He grabbed his backpack. "See you at baseball practice!" he cried, and sprinted down the hall.

"Amit, why are you taking the computer apart again? You know you're not supposed to do that. Besides, I thought we were going to work on our research together."

"Well, I was waiting for you and when you didn't show up, I started researching. Now, I'm finished. But you should've been here. The computer started making this sound like whirr-whirr, almost like the drives were overloaded. So I ripped out the motherboard and . . . "

"Wait, wait, what do you mean you're finished?" Davy asked.

"Mine was pretty easy. My family has been in India for generations and generations. As a matter of fact, my dad's visa was supposed to be for three years, but the computer company really needed him."

5

Davy's thoughts wandered back to Carlos. Maybe Carlos's dad could work for a computer company and then his family could stay.

Beep-beep. Amit opened his phone and smiled.

"Who's texting you? Your girlfriend?" Davy teased.

"Actually, it's my cousin Rajeev in Mumbai. We are meeting tonight via webcam to discuss algorithms and—" The bell rang, interrupting Amit. Davy could feel his stomach tying itself in knots as he realized that the afternoon was almost over, he still had baseball practice, and he hadn't even started his research yet.

After the final bell had rung, Davy, Carlos, Amit, and the rest of the Ballard Vikings huddled around Coach to hear his latest pep talk. "Okay, boys. Next week we're playing the Fremont Trolls, and they're a tough bunch. We've got to step it up; we've got to be motivated." Coach took a ragged breath and looked each boy in the face. "I've been reading about this new technique I want us to try. I want you to think about your favorite baseball hero. I want you to eat, breathe, and spit Hero."

Davy and Carlos secretly glanced at each other and stifled a laugh. They each knew just who the other was thinking of. Amit looked at his kinetic watch, wishing practice was over.

"First batter up is Carlos," Coach barked. "Amit, right field," he ordered. Amit grimaced.

"Good luck, Carlos," Davy whispered.

"And Davy, you're on deck."

Carlos picked up the bat, and took a practice swing with his eyes closed.

"Carlos, wake up! Here comes the ball!" Davy yelled.

As Carlos opened his eyes, the bat struck the seams. The ball sailed into right field. It caught the edge of Amit's mitt and rolled right down the line. "I'd much rather be playing cricket," Amit muttered under his breath as he scrambled for the ball. "Why does my dad make me play baseball?"

"That's it, Carlos! A double. Now, Davy, you're up," Coach grunted.

Davy walked up to the batter's box. *Eat, breathe, and spit Hero. Eat, breathe, and spit Hero*, he chanted to himself, and spat on the plate. As Davy looked up, the ball came hurtling through the strike zone.

"Come on, Davy! Focus!" Carlos shouted.

Eat, breathe, and spit Hero; eat, breathe, and spit Hero, Davy chanted and spat again. But this time, he kept his eye on the ball and smashed it over the fence. "It worked! It worked!" Davy yelled, as he and Carlos ran all the way home.

"Great job, boys. That's what we've got to do 'gainst the Trolls!" Coach roared.

As Davy opened the front door, he could hear his dad and brother cheering on the Seattle Mariners. "Hurry, Davy! You've got to see this. *Ichiro* is up to bat!" Michael squealed in excitement.

Davy rushed into the living room as Ichiro swung, striking the ball into the stands. "Homerun! Homerun! Just like me!" When Davy was up to bat, he was thinking of Ichiro. He wondered which hero Ichiro was eating, breathing, and spitting.

"Yeah right, Davy. You didn't hit a homerun. You couldn't hit the broad side of a school bus." Michael pretended to laugh.

"Michael, stop teasing your younger brother. I'm trying to watch the game," their dad said, turning up the volume.

Just then their mom came into the living room, wiping the guacamole from her hands with a dish towel. "What is this commotion about?"

"I did hit a homerun, and Michael doesn't believe me."

"Okay, stop you two. Taco bar is in the kitchen; go serve yourselves."

"Mmm . . . my favorite!" Davy exclaimed, as Michael pushed him aside to beat him into the kitchen.

"Enough, Michael! You're doing the dishes tonight," their mom said in a strict voice. Davy waited until her back was turned before sticking his tongue out at his brother.

Dinner came and went. Soon Davy was yawning. His stomach was full, it was the ninth inning, and he had had a very exciting day on the field. He stretched out on the couch, staring at the trophy shelf. Last year's Little League trophy glistened, and Davy remembered how he and Carlos had led the team to victory. How will we ever win the Little League tournament without Carlos? he thought.

Suddenly Davy remembered his project. He couldn't believe that he had gotten so caught up in the Mariners game that he had forgotten all about it. If I fail I won't be able to play baseball. His eyebrows scrunched in worry. "Mom, when did our family come to America?" he called out in a panic.

Davy's mom came down the stairs, out of the home office and said, "I really don't remember all the details." She scratched her head. "But I think our first ancestor to immigrate was from England. He was a judge or something. I saw a picture of him once and he was wearing a periwig."

Davy made a face. "What's a *periwig*?"

"It's like, well, it's kind of . . . " She fished something out of her pocket. "It's this." She handed Davy a quarter, heads up.

"Tell me more! Tell me more!"

"We will have to ask Grandma and Grandpa for the whole story."

"Can we call them now?" Davy pleaded.

She looked at the clock and said, "No, it's too late on the East Coast. They're asleep, and it's bedtime for you, too." She gently guided him to his bedroom.

"But I need to know where our family is from and if . . . " Davy persisted.

"Davy, I don't have time for these shenanigans. I have a big meeting early in the morning." She turned down the sheets for him and left the room.

Davy set his family tree on his nightstand and settled in with his steady old teddy. Sure, he was getting too old to sleep with a stuffed animal, and Michael was always reminding him of that, but he still liked to talk to his trusty friend. "Teddy, we've got to get up early and finish this tree. And what are we going to do about Carlos?" The bear didn't reply, but Davy felt at ease.

As the sun made its way up into the sky, Davy made his way down the school bus aisle. His shoes weren't tied, his backpack wasn't zipped, and his hair wasn't combed. He hated being the last one on the bus because that meant he'd have to sit up front with Mei Xing, or "Macy" as she demanded they call her. She talked more than *ten* teachers.

"Hi, Davy. Come sit by me!" Mei Xing yelled, waving her family tree. "How's your tree? Huh, how's it coming? Mine's all done, yep, all finished. It only took me three hours—two for research, one for coloring!"

Davy's eyes widened. His had taken only fifteen minutes! The alarm never went off, he'd overslept, and all he could do was scribble in his parents' and grandparents' names and flags. I need a good grade on this to keep pitching, he thought. His arm swung around just thinking about the fastballs he'd throw to Carlos as his eyes scanned the rows for his best friend.

But his best friend was already sitting at the back of the bus with Amit. He could see them laughing and gesturing wildly. They're probably sharing their families' exciting immigration adventures, he thought. I only have this silly story about a wig and a quarter. He sank down in the seat next to Mei Xing.

"Davy! Davy, are you listening to me?"

"What? Yes. Wow, Macy, sounds like you wrote a whole book on your family."

13

"Hardly. But I could have. My family members are so fascinating. Some of my ancestors migrated from Korea to China, and we emigrated from China to America because of my mother's groundbreaking experiments. Once, she got a formula all mixed up because I erased a little '2.' There was smoke everywhere and I even had to call the fire department. The fireman said, 'We need to get to the root of this!' But I told him, 'Not the root, the square!'"

Mei Xing talked, talked, and *talked* about her family, but Davy wasn't really listening. Disheartened, he leaned his head against the seat. He could overhear the two girls from Africa talking, but couldn't quite make out what they were saying over Mei Xing's chattering and the bus's rumbling. It sounded as if one of them said, "I'm a citizen now and not an *alien*. I'm so glad we won the green card lottery." Great, he thought, that story has lotteries and aliens. The class will eat it up like sweet cake. His mind began to wander: Did my family have adventures? How long has my family been in America? The bus lurched to a halt, and Davy knew he would not have a chance to look up the answers to these questions.

The school day had begun. Ms. Fortuna peered at her pupils over her black, cat-like glasses as she said, "Today we are going to learn about immigration from each other. We'll hear about adversity and diversity. And some of you will present your family trees to the class."

Maybe she won't call on me. Davy crossed his fingers. Please, please, please, he thought.

Ms. Fortuna's giant earrings were swinging up and down on her earlobes like monkeys on a rope. "Let's hear from Selam first."

"Whew," Davy let out his breath with relief.

Selam gracefully walked to the front of the class and waited for everyone to quiet down. Her beautiful green eyes fixed on the American flag as she began to speak, "I was living in a little village in the Sudan where all my family lived for hundreds of years. I have such happy memories of the warm sunshine, eating mangoes and papayas from the trees, and playing with my cousins. I also had some daily chores in the village, like helping with the dishes and collecting eggs for breakfast. Now that we are here, sometimes I go to work with my mom and dad at Pike Place Market. I pretend I'm doing chores for the village when I help out in the other stalls."

"If you liked it so much, why did your family leave?" Sophie asked.

Selam took a deep breath, stared at the flag, and said, "If we stayed, we might have died. One night a group of men burned down our village, and we had to flee to a refugee camp. We had to leave some of our family behind." Her eyes started tearing up. "I really miss my cousins, but for us to be free and safe we had to come to America."

Davy's eyes widened. He couldn't believe that someone he knew, a kid even, could have been killed.

Selam sighed and continued, "We were so scared when we first got here. We couldn't speak English, we didn't know *anybody*, and we had no money, but America took us in."

"Class, please give Selam a round of applause for sharing such a brave and fascinating story," Ms. Fortuna said.

15

Davy started to sweat. He really didn't have a story to tell. Selam and Macy have such interesting families compared to mine, he thought. Please don't let Ms. Fortuna call on me; he crossed his fingers again.

"Reginald, please share your family history," Ms. Fortuna said.

Davy whispered to himself, "Second time lucky."

Reggie was at his desk going over his project and carefully mouthing the words he'd prepared for class. He walked to the front and took center stage. "Ahem-ahem, ahem." He cleared his throat three times to get everyone's attention. "My *Family Tree and History*, by Reggie Hughes," he began, eyeing his classmates to make sure they were watching his performance.

"My family did immigrate to America, but not by choice. They did not want to leave Africa, but they were kidnapped." He paused for dramatic effect. "What I do know is that my great-great-great-*great*-grandparents were brought over on ships against their will and forced to work in the cotton fields. Grandma says we were lucky though, because our ancestors escaped." He paused again.

Create your family tree of flags

When did your family immigrate to America and why?

"Then, they integrated with an Indian tribe. Today, we call these people 'Native Americans' because they were the *first* Americans. Some believe they crossed the Bering Strait, which connected North America and Asia many thousands of years ago." He paused a third time to emphasize that neither side immigrated the way others' ancestors had. "I'm a Black Native American. You know, like that dude they made a statue of playing the guitar left-handed on Capitol Hill."

Amit raised his hand to get Reggie's attention. "So, how did your family end up in Seattle?"

"Excellent question!" he announced to the class. "In the 1950s we were part of the Second Great Migration from the South to the West." With that, Reggie swept his arms out in a regal bow. The class applauded his well-researched report.

"Wonderful, Reginald. You have a very special family history and a unique immigration, non-immigration, and migration story!"

Davy was chewing his fingernails. *My story only includes my parents and grandparents. My classmates will think it's so not exciting.* But before he could cross his fingers and say "third time's a charm," Ms. Fortuna said, "David, you're up!"

He knew he hadn't researched his family the way Reggie had. "There's only one thing left to do," Davy told himself. "Make it up!"

"My family tree and story, er, uh, I mean *history*." Davy eyed Ms. Fortuna to see if she had heard his mistake. But she just smiled patiently.

He stuck his hands in his pockets to hide his nervousness. His fingers touched metal, a quarter. "My family lived in England for thousands of years. They spoke with a British accent, wore periwigs, had high tea, and played a sport similar to baseball called 'cricket.'" Davy continued in a hurry. "My great-great-great-grandfather was an explorer and wanted to discover different places. He set sail on the open sea in search of a new land."

Davy looked around the classroom. One student was yawning. Another was whispering to his friend. *It's got to be more exciting,* he thought. He scanned the room for inspiration, and there it was—a ship.

Create your family tree of flags

Pirates, yes, pirates! he thought.

"But he was ambushed by pirates." The class gasped. "And they weren't just any buccaneers. They were baseball player pirates. They were the Pittsburgh Pirates!" A few kids choked on their spit. Ms. Fortuna waved her arms to quiet them down.

She calmly said, "David, could you please tell us when your family came to America?"

Davy blanked. He needed a date, any date. His mouth fumbled out the first number that came to mind: "1492."

"Hey Davy," a kid yelled, "who's your great-great-great-grandpa? Christopher Columbus?" The class burst out in laughter.

"Quiet, everyone," Ms. Fortuna said. "David, let's step outside for a second." She shut the door behind them. "That sounded like quite an adventurous story about someone else."

"But my family is *from* America, and all my friends have such interesting stories about how they got here. I'm just a plain old American." Davy sighed.

"Why do you say *plain old American?*" Ms. Fortuna asked, putting her arm around Davy's shoulders.

"Because I don't have a brave story like Selam's, or a unique story like Reggie's."

"I don't believe that, so I'm giving you another chance. You know, David, every American has an immigration story, and many have a relative who came through Ellis Island in New York. Do the research, leave no stone unturned, and you may be surprised at what you will discover."

Davy took Ms. Fortuna's advice to heart. He searched through the library stacks, trying to find anything on the Brown family. "Ten books so far, and nothing," he grumbled.

"Don't look so down; it's not the end of the world. At least Ms. Fortuna gave you another chance," Erika said, as she and Selam sat down at his table.

"Easy for you to say. I'm sure your story is more colorful than mine, and it's much easier for you to dig up your roots." He didn't mean to sound gruff—after all, he really liked Erika. But he was still burning from embarrassment, and to top it off, she'd seen the whole thing.

"Wait a minute. Think about where I'm from," Erika said with a smile.

Davy closed his book and said, "You're from South Africa."

"And?" she prompted.

He didn't understand what she was getting at.

"Look at me and look at Selam. We're from the same continent."

Suddenly, it dawned upon Davy that Erika didn't look like what he would imagine an African to look like.

"My ancestors immigrated to Africa in the seventeenth century from Europe. I miss Africa. I miss the African sun, the beautiful beaches, the lions, the giraffes, and the baboons."

"Baboons? Cool. You're from such an exotic place." He tried to imagine what it would be like to have monkeys in his backyard.

Erika twirled her hair around her finger, flattered by the compliment. "*Baie dankie.*"

"Huh? Buy a donkey?" Davy stared at her.

The two girls giggled. "It means, *thank you very much*, silly." Erika's eyes twinkled. "The monkeys were so naughty—my grandpa was always chasing them out of the house." She laughed at the memory. "But, luckily, he doesn't have to do that anymore. My grandparents moved here permanently because they missed me too much! I'm glad they did, because they really helped me with my family tree."

"Whenever I had a question back in the village, I always asked my grandparents," Selam said. "Grandparents have a very long memory."

"Today was the worst day of my life," Davy moaned. "I embarrassed myself in front of the whole class. And I still don't know how I will get this done." He looked down the street, hoping to see the bus in sight.

"Stop being so dramatic," Sophie said, looking at her watch. "I wonder if my new au pair got lost. She's five minutes late, and I need to finish my family tree."

Carlos glared at Sophie. He turned to Davy, "You are the star pitcher of the Ballard Vikings. You can always figure out how to throw a strike."

"Yeah, has the star found out *anything*? About his *real* family members, that is?" Sophie asked with an impish grin.

Davy could see his classmates biting their cheeks to keep from smiling.

"Not much luck. What about you, Sophie? Are you American?" Davy asked.

"Yeah, why?"

"I heard your mom talk, and she had a funny accent. She said, *"ello, Davy. Zhe weazher is magneefeesant, non?"*"

"That's because she's French. Duh." Sophie rolled her eyes at Davy.

"That seems strange. You're American, but your mom is French?"

"I don't know, Davy. Sounds like it could be true," Sophie said in a mocking tone.

She's such a smart aleck, Davy thought. "What about your dad? Does he say, '*magneefeesant*' too?"

Exasperated, she dropped the heavy backpack off her shoulder. It hit the ground, spitting up mud.

"It's like this. My dad is American. But he used to work in Paris—that's France, dummies—and it just so happened that he met the most beautiful woman in front of the Louvre Museum. My mother, of course. And they fell in love." Sophie puckered her lips. "Mwah-mwah."

"Yuck! Stupid love story," Amit said.

"Who would go to Paris to fall in love?" Carlos asked.

"My dad. That's who," Sophie snapped. "But his job brought him back to America. My dad really missed my mom, and my mom really missed my dad."

"I know what that's like," Mei Xing cut in. "My mom came to America before us, and my dad cried for her all the time."

"Okay, okay, enough mushy-gushy-wushy. Then what happened?" Davy asked.

Sophie huffed. "*Then*, they got engaged, my mom moved to America, they got married, and had a baby. A beautiful American girl who can speak English and French." Sophie winked at Mei Xing. The boys made faces and puking noises.

"Look, Davy, if you really want to get this done you need to ask your parents. But make sure you ask the right questions. You must be exact, *specific*, and that's not *Pacific*, like the ocean. Parents can be so thick-skulled sometimes." Sophie rolled her eyes.

"Don't forget to google your family too!" Amit added. He liked putting in his two cents.

Finally, Davy's bus pulled up. He ran up the stairs and looked back. "Enjoy your frog legs for dinner!" he cried, grinning. Hah! He'd gotten the last word on Sophie after all.

The bus dropped Davy and Carlos off at the usual spot, three blocks from Davy's house. Davy wished he was going to the field to practice with Carlos, but tonight he had to solve the puzzle of his family tree. It's not every day you get a second chance, he thought.

"You ready for the Trolls?" Carlos asked.

"You think your dad can get a job with Amit's dad's company?" Davy replied, his voice full of concern.

Carlos stopped in his tracks. "What? Why? That's out of left field."

"You're my best friend, and you're talking about maybe having to go back to Mexico. I really don't want you to leave. Besides, we could never beat the Trolls without you."

Carlos beamed. "Oh, Davy. You worry too much. We applied for our green cards. We hope they get approved. Then we'll be able to stay."

Davy's face lit up. "So you're not going to leave?"

"I hope not. Besides, I don't plan on letting my team get the snot beat out of them by a bunch of mangy trolls."

28

When Davy walked into the house, his father was already home watching a soccer match. "Come on, Beckham, go for the goal!" His dad jumped up, knocking the laundry off his lap.

What was Sophie telling me? Davy tried to remember. Oh yeah, I need to ask the right questions. I need to be *specific*. "Dad, do you know when our family came to America and where they came from? I need to create our family tree. I need to know when we immigrated and why we came," he said, trying to be as *specific* and Sophie-like as possible.

"I'm watching the game. Why don't you go ask your mom?"

"Please, Dad. I really need your help," Davy pleaded.

His dad set the laundry aside. "Let's go see what we can find on the Internet."

It worked! Davy thought. I asked the right questions and now we are getting somewhere. "Amit suggested that I google my family."

His mom was already in the home office, paying bills online. "Mom, will you unlock my Internet account?"

"I'm in the middle of something," she replied, clicking away.

Davy thought about Sophie's advice again. "I have to create our family tree of flags. You know—the project we started last night—and my deadline is tomorrow."

"Just one second," she said, logging off. "Why don't you start while I help Dad fold the laundry?" His parents walked out hand in hand.

Davy could not wait to find out where his family came from. Let's start googling Brown and New York, he thought. Two hundred million results came up. Way too many! Maybe Brown, New York, and Ellis Island would have better luck? Hmm, a little better at six hundred thousand. He started reading through the results and got to the Ellis Island website. Wow! What a cool website. He could type in the passenger name and even see the name of the ship. He bounded down the stairs. He was on his way to solving the puzzle.

"Dad, do you know who came to America first from your side of the family?" he gasped, out of breath.

"It was my great-great-grandfather, Lucas Brown."

Davy sprinted back to the computer, almost tripping on the stairs.

"Slow down," his mom warned.

He eagerly typed: Lucas Brown. No records. That can't be, he thought. I was sure I was on the right track. It was like throwing a strike only to have the ump call a ball.

"Davy!" his dad yelled from the living room. "I think my great-great-grandpa changed the spelling of his first and last names from L-U-K-A-S B-R-A-U-N to L-U-C-A-S B-R-O-W-N!"

A question mark crossed Davy's face. "Why did he change it?!" he yelled back.

"Easier to pronounce!" boomed up the stairs.

When did your family immigrate to America and why?

Davy crossed his fingers as he tried to type "Lukas Braun." He closed his eyes before he clicked "search" . . . and there it was: the whole passenger record listing his nationality, port of departure, manifest line number, the name of the ship he arrived on, and even a photo of the ship itself. It felt as if he'd gotten a strike out.

But there was still his mom's side of the family to research. Davy tried to think about all of his friends and their stories. How did they dig up the roots of their family trees? Amit suggested the Internet, Carlos the library, and Sophie and Macy got help from their parents. Who was he missing? Selam, Reggie, and Erika! They had all mentioned their grandparents and something about long memories.

Davy raced back to the living room. "I think we need Grandma. Can we call her now?"

"Sure!" his mom replied. Picking up her cell phone, she ordered it to "call Grandma," and handed the phone to Davy as it dialed.

"Hi Grandma! It's Davy."

"Good, good," Davy said.

"Yep, I've been eating, breathing, and spitting Hero. I hit a homerun at practice, and I'll do it again against the Trolls next week."

"Grandma, I need your help to fill in the branches of our family tree. When and why did the O'Briens come over?" Davy's grandma started from the beginning . . .

"Uh-huh." He shook his head in amazement. "I've never heard of a *potato famine*." He was taking notes at the speed of light.

"They discovered gold!" he exclaimed. So my ancestors were explorers after all, he thought.

Davy's face clouded over. "Did one of my ancestors really escape the Holocaust?" he breathed into the phone. It was hard to imagine his family had to flee just like Selam's.

"Of course I believe you, Grandma!" When Davy got off the phone, he returned to the computer and found the family members his grandmother told him about. There was only one thing left to do: color in the flags on his family tree.

The next morning at school, Davy couldn't wait to give his presentation.

"Good morning, everyone. Today we will hear all about David's family, or let's say the *real* story of David's family," Ms. Fortuna announced to the class.

Davy slowly walked to the front of the class and took center stage. A mischievous grin spread across his face as he pulled his family tree out of his social studies book. The class gasped. Davy's tree was the most colorful of them all: not only were there flags from Germany, Italy, Russia, the United Kingdom, Sweden, and Ireland, but there was also a totem pole, and the American flag was in the center.

Davy told stories from the eighteenth century until 1945, when his last family member immigrated. He showed their passenger records and photos from Ellis Island, the Gateway to America. They came to start a new life, a better life for everyone to come. Davy looked at his classmates and Ms. Fortuna with a big smile on his face, and said,

"In the words of Franklin D. Roosevelt: 'Remember, remember always that all of us, and you and I especially, are descended from immigrants and revolutionists.'"

Discussion Questions

1. Do you know why people immigrate to America?
   Hint: Look at the stories of Davy's friends and family.

2. Can you name any famous immigrants?
   Hint: Try to find the clues to famous immigrants throughout the book.

3. What is your favorite meal, and do you know where it originated?
   Hint: There are several examples of ethnic food in the book.

4. Do you know what the difference is between an immigrant and a nonimmigrant?
   Hint: Compare Erika, who is living in America permanently, to Estella, who will return to her home country.

5. Do you know what a green card is?
   Hint: Carlos's family applied for their green cards in order to stay in America.

6. Do you know what the difference is between emigration, immigration, and migration?
   Hint: Look at the stories of Mei Xing and Reggie.

7. Do you know what the difference is between an alien from outer space and a U.S. alien?
   Hint: While on the bus Davy hears Erika and Selam mention an "alien."

8. Do you know what a refugee is?
   Hint: See Selam's story.

9. Why do you think people changed the spelling of their names when they immigrated to America?
   Hint: Davy's dad gave one answer to this question.

10. Do you know where your family emigrated from?
    Hint: Try the same resources as Davy to discover your roots!

Please visit www.keelyvelani.com
for detailed answers and to order
your own family tree of flags.

Examples of Visas and Paths to Citizenship Featured in the Story

Carlos's dad is an example of a TN visa holder, who changed his status to H-1B in order to pursue permanent residency.

TN Visa: This type of nonimmigrant visa is available to citizens of Canada and Mexico for employment in certain professional occupations under the NAFTA agreement.

Estella's dad is an example of an H-2A visa holder.

H-2A Visa: This type of nonimmigrant visa is available to foreign nationals for temporary or seasonal agricultural work.

Amit's dad is an example of an H-1B visa holder.

H-1B Visa: This type of nonimmigrant visa is available to foreign nationals for employment in "specialty occupations." Those are occupations that require a bachelor's degree or higher. Although this is a nonimmigrant visa, the H-1B holder can have "dual intent." The H-1B holder may intend to either return to their home country or pursue permanent residency.

Mei Xing's mom was an O-1 visa holder who later obtained her green card.

O-1 Visa: This type of nonimmigrant visa is available to foreign nationals with extraordinary abilities in the sciences, arts, education, business, or athletics, or extraordinary achievements in the motion picture and television field.

Selam's family was resettled in the United States as refugees and later obtained their green cards.

Refugees are people who have fled their home countries because of persecution or fear of persecution. The United Nations High Commissioner for Refugees helps to coordinate refugee assistance with the help of many non-governmental organizations at troubled locations around the world. Individuals who have arrived in the United States by some other means may apply for political asylum.

Erika's parents won the green card lottery, were granted permanent residency, and later became citizens.

Diversity Lottery Program: The intent of this program is to diversify America. Every year a certain number of visas is set aside for countries with low rates of immigration to the United States.

Erika's grandparents were granted permanent residency.

Citizens can sponsor immediate relatives for family-based immigration. In this instance, Erika's parents sponsored her grandparents.

Sophie's au pair is an example of a J-1 visa holder.

J-1 Visa: This type of nonimmigrant visa is available for educational and cultural exchange programs, to foster understanding between the people of the United States and other countries.

Sophie's mom is an example of a K-1 visa holder who was granted permanent residency and later became a citizen.

K-1 Visa: This type of nonimmigrant visa is issued to the fiancé of an American citizen in order to enter the United States to get married, commonly referred to as the "fiancé visa."

For more detailed visa explanations and a comprehensive list of visas and immigration options, please visit
www.uscis.gov, www.unitedstatesvisas.gov, and **www.travel.state.gov**.
This book and its contents do not constitute legal advice and must not be used as a substitute for the advice of an immigration attorney.

The American Immigration Council

(formerly the American Immigration Law Foundation) is a tax–exempt not-for-profit educational, charitable organization dedicated to increasing public understanding of the value of immigration to American society, and to advancing fundamental fairness and due process under the law for immigrants.

The **American Immigration Council's Curriculum Center** serves as a national clearinghouse and resource for teaching immigration history and policy to grades K–12. The Curriculum Center sponsors the annual 5th Grade Creative Writing Contest, funds community and classroom service learning projects, provides training to educators to encourage innovative teaching techniques, and produces an annual resource guide that is distributed widely.

Get Interactive with the American Immigration Council!

5th Grade Creative Writing Contest

"Why I'm Glad America is a Nation of Immigrants"

Open to fifth grade students across the nation. The Grand Prize winner receives an all-expenses paid trip to the American Immigration Council's Annual Benefit Dinner, to be honored and to read the winning entry aloud. In addition, the winner receives an engraved plaque; the winning entry is printed in the Congressional Record; and a flag is flown over the Capitol in the winner's honor. For contest details, please visit:

www.americanimmigrationcouncil.org

Immigration Nation—American Immigration Council's Student Blog!

Instead of building borders around this controversial topic, Immigration Nation serves as a platform where students can freely express their immigration experience and communicate with educators. Join Immigration Nation and tell your immigration story or share your thoughts on immigration. Let's get talking!

Visit *www.immigrationnation.org*, sign up, and start blogging today!

Additional Resources

The African-American Migration—Schomberg Center for Research in Black Culture
http://www.inmotionaame.org/home.cfm;jsessionid=f8302496761233567281364?bhcp=1

Angel Island
http://www.angelisland.org/immigr02.html

Ellis Island
http://www.ellisisland.org

Immigration Nation
http://www.teachimmigration.org

The Learning Page—Part of the American Memory Collection
http://lcweb2.loc.gov/ammem/ndlpedu/features/immig/immigration_set1.html

Lower East Side Tenement Museum
http://www.tenement.org/

Online Genealogy Records
http://www.ancestry.com/

PBS Kids—Big Apple History
http://pbskids.org/bigapplehistory/immigration/index-flash.html

Scholastic—Immigration Stories of Yesterday and Today
http://teacher.scholastic.com/activities/immigration/